Webster
the World's

by Sheila L
Illustrated by John Ireland

Lucy Lemon had two cats, three rabbits,
seven guinea-pigs and a budgie who sang
"Knees Up Mother Brown".

She had a hamster called Henry and
a goldfish called Josh the Splosh.

She had a tortoise called Rover who didn't like going for walks …

4

... and she had six white mice
who did.

What Lucy didn't have was a dog.

One Sunday, Lucy and her family went for a
walk. Dad went in front with Mum and Gran.
Tom and Sally came next, with Kate in her
push-chair.
Last of all came Lucy, with Rover on his lead.

They walked down Holly Lane towards the
sea. A notice on a wire fence said
GIVE A DOG A HOME.
"We could do that," said Lucy.
"There's no harm in going in,"
said Dad.

GIVE A
DOG
A HOME

HOLLY
LANE
DOG
RESCUE

So in they went.

They saw big dogs and small dogs,
bald dogs and hairy dogs, dogs with tails
and dogs without.

"What about a quiet little spaniel?" said Mum.

"A poodle," said Gran.

"A retriever," said Tom.

"A German shepherd," said Sally.

"I like this one," said Lucy.

The keeper came by with some bowls of food.
"That's Webster," she said.
"He's the worst dog in the world.
He's so big and bouncy, nobody
can handle him.
Everybody brings him back."
"We'll look at something else,"
            said Mum hastily.

10

"I like Webster best," said Lucy.

"So do I," said Tom and Sally together.

"So do I," said Gran.

"I'm sure I could train him," said Dad.

"Let's give him a try."

The keeper unlocked the cage.
"Don't say I didn't warn you," she said.
Webster bounded out joyfully.

On the way home, Lucy went in front with
Webster on his lead. Tom and Sally came
next, with Kate in her push-chair.
Next came Dad and Gran.
Last of all came Mum, carrying Rover.

The cats were on the wall outside, washing their paws in the sunshine. "WOOF!" said Webster, and chased them up the apple tree.

"Bad dog, Webster!"
shouted Lucy.
"SIT, Webster,"
ordered Dad.

Webster raced
around the garden,
barking at the birds.

"Bad dog, Webster!"
shouted Tom and Sally.
"STAY, Webster!" bellowed Dad.

Webster jumped in the fishpond.
SPLASH! The water went
all over Mum.

"Bad dog, Webster!" shouted Mum.
"HEEL, Webster!" yelled Dad.

Webster dug a hole in the vegetable patch.
Carrots and onions went
flying through the air.

Gran was showered with soil.
"Bad dog, Webster!" shouted Gran.
"DOWN, Webster!" thundered Dad.

Webster galloped into the house and up the stairs. He dragged the covers from Lucy's bed. He dropped Dad's slippers in the loo. He chewed up Gran's geraniums, and he made a puddle on the bathroom floor.

"BAD DOG, WEBSTER!" shouted everybody.

When evening came they were all worn out.
Webster went to sleep in the laundry basket,
on a pile of clean sheets.
"It's no use," sighed Mum.
"Webster is impossible.
First thing in the morning,
we'll have to take him back."

They sat down for supper and the house was quiet at last.

Bertie the budgie dozed peacefully on his perch.

Nobody heard next door's cat slink silently through the open window.

Nobody saw him creeping towards Bertie's cage.

Nobody but Webster.

The cat pounced, but Webster
pounced too.
The cage crashed to the floor.
Webster barked, the cat squalled,
and Bertie screeched in fright.
"Good grief!" said Dad.
"Whatever's going on?"

The cat fled down the garden.
"HE won't be back in a hurry!"
said Dad, shutting the window.
"He almost got Bertie," said Mum.
"It's lucky Webster was here."
"Knees Up Mother Brown!" chirped Bertie,
fluttering his feathers into place.

Everybody patted Webster's head.
"Good old Webster," said Tom and Sally.
"He saved Bertie's life," said Gran.
"We can't send him back now," said Lucy.
"Can we, Dad?" Dad smiled.
"Let's give him another chance," he said.
"Maybe he's not such
a bad dog, after all."

Lucy put her arms round Webster's neck.
"He's the best dog in the world!" she said,
and Webster seemed to think so too.